This Book Belongs to:

_____

_____

GIANT TREASURY OF
BRER RABBIT

Retold from the Stories of
JOEL CHANDLER HARRIS

by ANNE HESSEY

Illustrated by HARRY ROUNTREE *and* RENÉ BULL

DERRYDALE BOOKS
New York • Avenel

For Meghan and Cooper

Random House
New York • Toronto • London • Sydney • Auckland

Printed and bound in the United States of America

Library of Congress Cataloging-in-Publication Data
Hessey, Anne,
Giant treasury of Brer Rabbit / retold from the stories of Joel Chandler Harris by Anne Hessey ;
illustrated by Harry Rountree and René Bull.
p.   cm.
Summary: A retelling of the classic Afro-American tales about Br'er Rabbit and his friends
and enemies, animals who are constantly on the prowl to fool each other.
ISBN 0-517-03293-7
1. Afro-Americans—Folklore. 2. Tales—United States.
[1. Folklore, Afro-American. 2. Animals—Folklore.] I. Harris, Joel Chandler, 1848-1908.
II. Rountree, Harry, b. 1878, ill. III. Bull, René, b. 1870, ill. IV. Title.
PZ8.1.H44Gi   1990
813'.4—dc 20 [398.2] [E] 90-49939 CIP AC

10 9 8 7 6 5 4 3

Book design by Jean Krulis
Cover design by Clair Moritz

CONTENTS

INTRODUCTION

Meet Brer Rabbit, Brer Fox, Brer Terrapin and the rest of the gang! These crafty characters outsmart each other and sometimes themselves, as they go from one adventure to another in a world full of tricks, triumphs, danger and disaster. Action is the name of the game and cleverness the key to winning. Both children and adults will tingle with suspense, laugh at the outrageous tricks, and sometimes wince, as they recognize things they see not only in others but also in themselves.

The locale is that of the rural American South, but the stories came originally from Africa. These folk tales tell of a day when "creatures had lots more sense than they have now; let alone that, they had sense like people." Brer Rabbit was "at the head of the gang when any racket" was going on, and he "and Brer Fox were like some children. Both of them were always after one another, pranking and pestering around."

The pictures by Harry Rountree and René Bull beautifully capture the characters of Brer Rabbit, the masterful trickster, persistent Brer Fox, wise and gentle Brer Terrapin, and all the rest of the animals. Their feelings and actions are shown clearly and amusingly, always faithful to the spirit of the stories. Seeing just the tips of Brer Fox's tail and nose, we still can tell what's going on in his head. And you'll see Brer Rabbit smug, angry, scared, jovial, surprised, crying crocodile tears, or genuinely dismayed.

Brer Rabbit, the chief trickster, simply cannot leave well enough alone. Neither can any of the rest of them: Brothers Fox, Wolf, Buzzard, Bullfrog, Terrapin, Possum, and Bear. They trick each other, they chase each other, they work together, and play together. While often they get brought down by their own greediness, sometimes "folks have to suffer for other folk's sins." They take turns winning and losing, but Brer Rabbit usually comes out on top: an agile mind wins out over brute strength.

At times, Brer Rabbit may seem like a Wicked Rabbit, but you will see, if you look carefully, that he's a Different Rabbit. These stories do not focus at all on the triumph of good over evil or on the need for punishment: they are African folklore, not European myth or legend. The stories deal with tricks for the sake of trickery, with outsmarting the other fellow, and with what happens when a creature succumbs to temptation too greedily for his own good. You'll learn strategies for winning both fairly and foully; you won't find a moral at the end of each story, but you can find plenty to discuss and think about.

Joel Chandler Harris, an American newspaperman and writer, collected these stories in 1880 under the title, *Uncle Remus: His Songs and His Sayings.* Harris wanted to capture for posterity the African tales told by the slaves on the cotton plantations in a written form completely faithful to the stories as he had heard them. As originally published, however, *Uncle Remus: His Songs and His Sayings* presents two problems for the modern reader.

First, Harris's strong and accurate use of dialect would make reading these stories extremely difficult today. One finds it hard to sit down with a child in one's lap and read aloud, "De way dat Brer Rabbit 'cieve Brer Fox done got to be de tak er der naberhood." Therefore, for this edition, we have modernized the language but have taken care to retain the character, rhythm, and color of the original stories.

Secondly, Harris used the character of Uncle Remus, the kindly old former slave telling stories to the little white boy from the "Big House," as a thread to tie the stories together. As the racial stereotypes of the nineteenth century are inappropriate today and may be offensive to many contemporary readers, we have eliminated the storytelling Uncle Remus and the little boy. The stories stand firmly on their own, in fact, as part of the African heritage which has enriched this country's culture, and their durability over the years testifies to the force of animal mythology which goes far back in time.

ANNE HESSEY

1991

About the Artists

The delightful illustrations were done by Harry Rountree and René Bull, book illustrators who worked in England primarily in the first quarter of this century. The full-page color plates are the work of Rountree, and the smaller line drawings are by Bull, originally done in black and white, but nearly half have been colored, specially for this edition.

CLAIRE BOOSS
Editor

Mr. Fox Tries to Trick Mr. Rabbit

One day after Brer Fox had done all that he could to catch Brer Rabbit, and Brer Rabbit had done all he could to keep him from it, Brer Fox said to himself that he'd play a trick on Brer Rabbit. He'd no more than got the words out of his mouth than Brer Rabbit came loping up the big road looking just as plump, and as fat, and as sassy as a prize horse in a barley-patch.

"Hold on there, Brer Rabbit," said Brer Fox.

"I've got no time, Brer Fox," said Brer Rabbit, sort of nervously.

"I want to talk some with you, Brer Rabbit," said Brer Fox.

"All right, Brer Fox, but you better holler from where you stand. I'm monstrous full of fleas this morning," said Brer Rabbit.

"I saw Brer Bear yesterday," said Brer Fox, "and he raked me over the coals because you and me don't make friends and live neighborly, and I told him that I'd see you."

Then Brer Rabbit scratched one ear sort of judiciously with his hind foot and said, "All right, Brer Fox. Suppose you drop around tomorrow and take dinner with me. We don't eat very fancy at our house, but I expect my wife and the children can scramble around and get up something to fill your stomach."

"I'm agreeable, Brer Rabbit," said Brer Fox.

"Then I'll depend on you," said Brer Rabbit.

The next day Mr. Rabbit and Mrs. Rabbit got up early, before daybreak, raided a garden and got some cabbages, some ears of corn, and some

asparagus, and they fixed a terrific dinner. By and by, one of the little Rabbits, playing out in the back yard, came running in, hollering, "Oh, Ma! Oh, Ma! I saw Mr. Fox a-coming!"

So Brer Rabbit took the children by their ears and made them sit down, then he and Mrs. Rabbit dallied around waiting for Brer Fox. They kept on waiting, but no Brer Fox came. After a while, Brer Rabbit went to the door quietly and peeped out, and there, sticking out from behind the corner, was the tip of Brer Fox's tail. Brer Rabbit shut the door and sat down, put his paws behind his ears and began to sing:

"The place whereabout you spill the grease,
  Right there you're bound to slide,
And where you find a bunch of hair,
  You'll surely find the hide."

The next day, Brer Fox sent word by Mr. Mink, and excused himself because he was too sick to come, and he asked Brer Rabbit to come and take dinner with him. Brer Rabbit said he was willing.

By and by, when the shadows were at their shortest, Brer Rabbit spruced himself up and sauntered down to Brer Fox's house. When he got there, he heard somebody groaning. He looked in the door and there he saw Brer Fox sitting in a rocking chair all wrapped up in flannel, looking mighty weak.

9

Brer Rabbit searched all around, but he saw no dinner. The dish pan was sitting on the table, and close by was a big, sharp knife.

"Looks like you're going to have chicken for dinner, Brer Fox," said Brer Rabbit.

"Yes, Brer Rabbit, they're nice and fresh and tender," said Brer Fox.

Then Brer Rabbit pulled his moustache and said, "You haven't got any calamus root, have you, Brer Fox? I've gotten now so that I can't eat any chicken unless it's seasoned with calamus root."

And with that, Brer Rabbit leapt out the door, dodged among the bushes, and sat there watching for Brer Fox. He didn't watch long, either, because Brer Fox flung off the flannel, crept out of the house and got where he could close in on Brer Rabbit. By and by, Brer Rabbit yelled out, "Oh, Brer Fox! I'll just put your calamus root out here on this stump. Better come get it while it's fresh!"

And with that, Brer Rabbit galloped off home. Brer Fox hasn't caught him yet, and what's more, he's never going to.

The Wonderful Tar Baby Story

One day after Brer Rabbit fooled Brer Fox with that calamus root, Brer Fox decided he was going to get even. He went to work and got himself some tar, mixed it with some turpentine, and fixed up a contraption that he called a Tar Baby. He took the Tar Baby and he set it in the middle of the big road, and then he lay down in the bushes to see what the news was going to be. He didn't have to wait long because, by and by, along came Brer Rabbit pacing down the road—lippity-clippity, clippity-lippity—just as sassy as a jaybird. Brer Fox lay low. Brer Rabbit came prancing along until

11

he spied the Tar Baby, and he stopped dead, and sat up on his hind legs in astonishment. The Tar Baby just sat there, and Brer Fox lay low.

"Morning!" said Brer Rabbit. "Nice weather this morning."

Tar Baby said nothing, and Brer Fox stayed hidden in the bushes.

"How are you feeling today?" asked Brer Rabbit.

Brer Fox winked his eye slowly and lay low, and the Tar Baby sat there, silent.

"How are you, then? Are you deaf?" asked Brer Rabbit. "Cause if you are, I can holler louder!"

Tar Baby stayed still, and Brer Fox lay low.

"You're stuck up, that's what you are," said Brer Rabbit, "and I'm going to cure you, that's what I'm going to do!"

Brer Fox sort of chuckled in his stomach, but Tar Baby still said nothing.

"I'm goin' to teach you how to talk to respectable folks, if it's my last act," said Brer Rabbit. "If you don't take off that hat and tell me howdy, I'm going to bust you wide open."

Tar Baby stayed still, and Brer Fox stayed in the bushes.

Brer Rabbit kept on asking, and the Tar Baby kept on saying nothing until, presently, Brer Rabbit drew back his fist, and—blip! He struck it on the side of the head! And right there's where he met trouble. His fist got stuck, and he couldn't pull loose: the tar held him fast. But even, then, the Tar Baby stayed still, and Brer Fox continued to hide.

"If you don't let me loose, I'll hit you again," said Brer Rabbit, and with

that, he gave it a smack with the other hand, and that stuck, too. Tar Baby said nothing, and Brer Fox lay low.

"Turn me loose, before I kick the natural stuffing out of you!" hollered Brer Rabbit, but the Tar Baby stayed perfectly quiet, just held on. And then Brer Rabbit lost the use of his feet in the same way. Brer Fox lay low and watched. Then Brer Rabbit squealed out that if the Tar Baby didn't turn him loose, he'd "butt the baby lopsided." So then he butted, and his head got stuck. At this point, Brer Fox sauntered forth, looking just as innocent as a tame mockingbird.

"Howdy, Brer Rabbit," said Brer Fox. "You look sorter stuck-up this morning," he said, and then he rolled on the ground and laughed and laughed until he could laugh no more. "I expect you'll take dinner with me this time, Brer Rabbit. I've laid in some calamus root, and I'm not taking any excuse," said Brer Fox.

And that's how the tale ends. Some say Judge Bear came along and loosened Brer Rabbit—and some say he didn't.

Why Mr. Possum Loves Peace

One night Brer Possum called for Brer Raccoon according to their custom, and after gobbling up a dish of fried greens and smoking a cigar, they rambled forth to see how the neighborhood was getting along. Brer Raccoon had a naturally easy gait, and paced along as smooth as a pony, while Brer Possum went in a slow gallop, so they covered a lot of ground. Brer Possum filled his belly full of plums, and Brer Raccoon scooped up an abundance of frogs and tadpoles. They ambled along, happy as a basket of kittens, till by and by, they heard Mr. Dog talking to himself, way off in the woods.

"Supposing he runs up on us, Brer Possum, what are you going to do?" asked Brer Raccoon. Brer Possum just laughed from the corners of his mouth.

"Oh, if he comes, Brer Raccoon, I'm going to stand by you," said Brer Possum. "What are you going to do?"

15

"Who? Me?" said Brer Raccoon. "If he runs up to me, I'll give him one good twist."

Suddenly, Mr. Dog came zooming in, and he didn't wait to say howdy, either: he just sailed into the two of them. The very first pass he made, Brer Possum grinned from ear to ear, and keeled over like he was dead. So Mr. Dog sailed into Brer Raccoon, and right there's where

he made his mistake, because Brer Raccoon was cut out for just that kind of business, and he fairly wiped up the face of the earth with him! You had better believe that when Mr. Dog got a chance to make himself scarce, he took it, and what there was left of him went skedaddling through the woods like a shot out of a gun. Then Brer Raccoon licked his clothes into shape and headed off, while Brer Possum lay there like he was dead, till, by and by, he raised up carefully and when he found the coast clear, he scrambled up and scampered off as fast as he could.

The next time Brer Possum met Brer Raccoon, his friend refused to answer his howdy, and this made Brer Possum feel mighty bad, seeing as how they used to make so many excursions together.

"What makes you hold your head so high, Brer Raccoon?" asked Brer Possum.

"I'm not running with cowards these days," said Brer Raccoon. "When I want to, I'll send for you," said he.

Then Brer Possum got mighty mad.

"Who's any coward?" said he.

"You are," said Brer Raccoon, "that's who. I don't associate with those who lay down on the ground and play dead when there's a free fight going on."

Then Brer Possum grinned and laughed fit to kill himself.

"My, my, Brer Raccoon, you don't expect I did that because I was afraid, do you?" said he. "Why I wasn't any more afraid than you are this minute. What was there to be scared of?" said he. "I knew you'd do away with Mr. Dog if I didn't, and I just lay there watching you shake him, waiting to help when the time came."

Brer Raccoon turned up his nose.

"That's a mighty likely tale," said he. "Why, when Mr. Dog no more than touched you, you keeled over, and lay there stiff."

"That's what I was going to tell you about," said Brer Possum. "I was no more scared than you are right now, and I was fixing to give Mr. Dog a sample of my jaw, but I'm the most ticklish chap that you ever laid eyes on, and no sooner did Mr. Dog put his nose down here among my ribs, than I got to laughing, and I laughed till I had no use of my limbs, and it's a mercy for Mr. Dog that I was ticklish, 'cause a little more, and I'd have eaten him up," said he. "I don't mind fighting, Brer Raccoon, no more than you do, but

I can't stand tickling. Get me in a row where there's no tickling allowed, and I'm your man."

And down to this day, Brer Possum's bound to surrender when you touch him in the short ribs, and he'll laugh even if he knows he's going to be smashed for it.

How Mr. Rabbit Was Too Sharp for Mr. Fox

In those days, Brer Rabbit and his family were right in the middle of things whenever any racket was going on, and there they stayed. Before you begin to wipe your eyes about Brer Rabbit, wait and see where Brer Rabbit ended up.

When Brer Fox found Brer Rabbit mixed up with the Tar Baby, he felt mighty good, and he rolled on the ground and laughed. By and by, he said,

"Well, I expect I got you this time, Brer Rabbit. Maybe I don't, but I think I do. You've been running around here sassing me for a long time, but I expect you've come to the end now! You've been cutting your capers and bouncing around this neighborhood until you've started to think you're the boss of the whole show. Besides, you're always somewhere you've got no business being," said Brer Fox. "Who asked you to come and strike up an acquaintance with the Tar Baby, anyway? And who got you stuck where you are now? Nobody in the whole wide world but you. You just went and jammed yourself onto that Tar Baby without waiting for any invite," sneered Brer Fox, "and there you are, and there you'll stay, till I fix up a brush pile and light it, 'cause I'm going to barbecue you this day, for sure!"

At that, Brer Rabbit spoke mighty humbly: "I don't care what you do with me, Brer Fox," he whimpered, "just so you don't fling me in that brier patch. Roast me, Brer Fox, but don't fling me in that brier patch."

"It's so much trouble to kindle a fire that I expect I'll have to hang you," said Brer Fox.

"Hang me just as high as you please, Brer Fox," begged Brer Rabbit, "but don't, for Heaven's sake, fling me in that brier patch!"

"I've got no string," said Brer Fox, "so now I expect I'll have to drown you."

"Drown me just as deep as you please, Brer Fox," moaned Brer Rabbit, "but please, please, PLEASE, don't fling me in that brier patch!"

"There's no water near, so now I expect I'll have to skin you," threatened Brer Fox.

Of course, Brer Fox wanted to hurt Brer Rabbit as much as he could, so he caught him by the hind legs and slung him right into the middle of the

brier patch. There was a considerable flutter where Brer Rabbit struck the bushes, and Brer Fox hung around to see what was going to happen. By and by, he heard somebody calling him, and way up the hill, he saw Brer Rabbit sitting cross-legged on a pine log, combing the tar out of his hair with a wood chip. Then Brer Fox knew that he'd been tricked, for sure. Brer Rabbit just had to sass him back, so he hollered out:

"Born and bred in a brier patch, Brer Fox—born and bred in a brier patch!" and with that, he skipped away just as lively as a cricket.

Mr. Rabbit Grossly Deceives Mr. Fox

After Brer Rabbit got loose from Brer Fox and the Tar Baby, he stayed pretty close to home until he got the tar out of his hair, but it wasn't long before he was loping up and down the neighborhood, sassy as ever.

The tale of how he mixed with the Tar Baby got around the neighborhood. At least Miss Meadows and the gals got wind of it, and the next time Brer Rabbit paid them a visit, Miss Meadows asked him about it, and burst out laughing. Brer Rabbit sat up just as cool as a cucumber and let them giggle as much as they wanted.

He was quiet as a lamb and, by and by, he crossed his legs, winked his eye slowly, and said, "Ladies, Brer Fox was my daddy's riding horse for thirty years, maybe more, but thirty years that I know of, for sure." Then he paid them his respects, tipped his hat, and marched off, just as stiff and stuck up as a poker. Next day, Brer Fox came calling, and, when he began to laugh about Brer Rabbit, Miss Meadows and the gals told him what Brer Rabbit said.

Brer Fox gritted his teeth and looked mighty grumpy, and when he rose to go, he said, "Ladies, I'm not disputing what you report, but I'll make Brer Rabbit chew up his words and spit them out right here where you can see him." And with that, off he went.

When he got onto the main road, he shook the dew from his tail and made straight for Brer Rabbit's house. Brer Rabbit was expecting him, so

the door was shut fast. Brer Fox knocked but nobody answered. So, he knocked again—Blam! Blam! Brer Rabbit hollered out weakly, "Is that you, Brer Fox? I want you to run and fetch the doctor. That parsley I ate this morning made me feel sick. Go, please, Brer Fox, run quick," said Brer Rabbit.

"I came to get you, Brer Rabbit," said Brer Fox. "There's going to be a party up at Miss Meadow's, and all the gals will be there. I promised that I'd fetch you. The gals say it won't be a party if I don't bring you."

Brer Rabbit claimed he was too sick, while Brer Fox swore he wasn't, and they argued the matter up and down, disputing and contending. Brer Rabbit said he couldn't walk. Brer Fox said he'd carry him. Brer Rabbit asked how? Brer Fox said in his arms. Brer Rabbit said he'd drop him. Brer Fox promised he wouldn't. By and by, Brer Rabbit said he would go if Brer Fox would carry him on his back, and Brer Fox agreed. But Brer Rabbit claimed he couldn't ride without a saddle, so Brer Fox promised to get a saddle. Next, Brer Rabbit said he couldn't sit in the saddle unless he had a bridle to hold, and Brer Fox offered to get a bridle. Brer Rabbit said he couldn't ride without a bridle with blinders, because Brer Fox would be shying at stumps along the road and fling him off, so Brer Fox even said he'd get a blind bridle. Finally, Brer Rabbit agreed to go! Brer Fox said he'd let Brer Rabbit ride almost up to Miss Meadow's, if he'd get down and walk the balance of the way, and Brer Rabbit agreed to that, so Brer Fox ran off to get the saddle and bridle.

Of course, Brer Rabbit knew the game that Brer Fox was playing, and he determined to outdo him. By the time he had combed his hair, twisted his mustache, and cleaned up, Brer Fox was back, wearing his saddle and bridle, looking as pert as a circus pony. He trotted up to the door and stood there pawing the ground and chomping the bit like an honest-to-goodness horse, and Brer Rabbit mounted and off they went. Brer Fox couldn't see behind him with the blind bridle on, but, by and by, he felt Brer Rabbit raise one of his feet.

"What you doing now, Brer Rabbit?" he asked.

"Shortening the left stirrup, Brer Fox."

Then Brer Rabbit raised up the other foot.

"What you doing now, Brer Rabbit?"

"Pulling down my pants, Brer Fox."

All this time, Brer Rabbit was putting on his spurs, and when they got close to Miss Meadows's where Brer Rabbit was to get off, Brer Fox came to a halt. With that, Brer Rabbit slapped the spurs into Brer Fox's flanks, and you better believe that Brer Fox moved mighty fast! When they got to the house, Miss Meadows and all the gals were sitting on the porch, but instead of stopping at the gate, Brer Rabbit rode on by, and then came galloping down the road and up to the horse rack. He hitched Brer Fox to it, sauntered into the house, and shook hands with the gals. Then he sat down and smoked his cigar, just like a gentleman.

By and by, he drew in a long puff, letting it out in a cloud, sat up straight, and hollered out, "Ladies, haven't I told you Brer Fox was the riding horse for our family? He's sort of losing his gait now, but I expect I can make him all right in a month or so."

Brer Rabbit grinned, the gals giggled, and Miss Meadows praised the pony. And there was Brer Fox, hitched fast to the rack, not able to do a blessed thing about it.

Mr. Fox Is Again Victimized

After Brer Rabbit had tied Brer Fox to the hitching post, he visited with Miss Meadows and the gals for a while. They talked, and they sang, and they played the piano, until, by and by, it came time for Brer Rabbit to leave. He bade them all good-by, and strutted out to the horse rack as if he were the king of the castle, mounted Brer Fox, and rode off.

Brer Fox said nothing at all. He just trotted off and kept his mouth shut, but Brer Rabbit knew there was something cooking, and he felt monstrous skittish. Brer Fox ambled on until he got out of sight of Miss Meadows's house, and then he turned loose! He ripped and he reared, and he cussed and he swore, he snorted and he cavorted.

He was trying to fling Brer Rabbit off of his back, but he might just as well have wrestled with his own shadow. Every time he bucked, Brer Rabbit slapped the spurs to him, and so on they went, up and down. Brer Fox fairly tore up the ground, jumping so high and so quick that he mighty near took his tail off. They kept on going this way until, by and by, Brer Fox had the clever idea to lie down and roll over, and this finally unsettled Brer Rabbit. By the time Brer Fox got back on his feet again, Brer Rabbit was

whipping through the underbrush like a racehorse. Brer Fox lit out after him and got so close that it was all Brer Rabbit could do to dart into a hollow tree. Fortunately for Brer Rabbit, the hole was too little for Brer Fox, so he lay down to rest and gather his thoughts together.

While he was lying there, Mr. Buzzard came flapping along, and seeing Brer Fox stretched out on the ground, he lit nearby. Mr. Buzzard shook his wings, put his head on one side, and murmured to himself, "Brer Fox is dead, and I'm so sorry."

"No, I'm not dead, either," said Brer Fox. "I got old man Rabbit penned up in this tree and I'm going to get him this time if it takes twelve Christmases."

After some more talk, Brer Fox made a bargain with Mr. Buzzard to watch the hole and keep Brer Rabbit there while Brer Fox went for his axe. Brer Fox loped off and Mr. Buzzard took up his stand at the hole in the tree. By and by, when all got quiet, Brer Rabbit scrambled down close to the hole and hollered out, "Brer Fox! Oh! Brer Fox!"

Brer Fox, of course, was gone, and Brer Buzzard stayed quiet. Then Brer

Rabbit yelled as if he was mad, "You needn't talk unless you want to. I know you're there, and I don't care. I just want to tell you that I wish mighty bad that Brer Turkey Buzzard were here," he said.

Then Mr. Buzzard tried to talk like Brer Fox, "What you want with Mr. Buzzard?" he asked.

"Oh, nothing in particular, except there's the fattest gray squirrel in here that ever I've seen," replied Brer Rabbit, "and if Brer Turkey Buzzard was around, he'd be mighty glad to get him."

"How is Mr. Buzzard going to get him?" asked the Buzzard.

"Well, there's a little hole round on the other side of the tree," said Brer Rabbit, "and if Brer Turkey Buzzard was here, he could take up his stand there, and I'd drive that squirrel out."

"Drive him out, then," shouted Mr. Buzzard "and I'll see that Brer Turkey Buzzard gets him."

Then Brer Rabbit kicked up a racket, pretending to drive something out, Mr. Buzzard rushed around to catch the squirrel, and Brer Rabbit dashed out and ran for home.

Mr. Fox Is Outdone by Mr. Buzzard

Mr. Turkey Buzzard was guarding the hollow where Brer Rabbit had hidden. He felt mighty lonesome, but he had promised Brer Fox that he'd stay, so he decided to hang around and join in the joke. He didn't have long to wait, because soon Brer Fox came galloping through the woods with his axe on his shoulder.

"How do you expect Brer Rabbit's getting on, Brer Buzzard?" asked Brer Fox.

"Oh, he's in there," answered Brer Buzzard. "He's mighty still, though. I expect he's taking a nap."

"Then I'm just in time to wake him up," said Brer Fox. And with that he flung off his coat, spit in his hands, and grabbed the axe. Then he drew

back and came down on the tree—pow! And every time he came down with the axe—pow!—Mr. Buzzard stepped high and hollered out, "Oh, he's in there, Brer Fox. He's in there, sure."

And every time a chip would fly off, Mr. Buzzard would jump and dodge, and hold his head sideways, and holler: "He's in there, Brer Fox. I heard him. He's in there, for sure."

Brer Fox lammed away at that hollow tree like a man splitting rails, until, by and by, after he got the tree 'most cut through, he stopped to catch his

breath. Then he saw Mr. Buzzard laughing behind his back and right then and there, without going any further, Brer Fox smelled a rat. But Mr. Buzzard kept on hollering: "He's in there, Brer Fox. He's in there sure. I saw him!"

Then Brer Fox pretended to peek up the hollow tree and said, "Run here, Brer Buzzard, and see if this isn't Brer Rabbit's foot hanging down here."

Mr. Buzzard came stepping up as if he were treading on prickles and stuck his head in the hole. No sooner had he done that than Brer Fox grabbed him. Mr. Buzzard flapped his wings and scrambled around as hard as he could, but it was no use—Brer Fox had the advantage and he held him right down to the ground.

Then Mr. Buzzard screamed, "Let me alone, Brer Fox. Turn me loose! Brer Rabbit'll get out. You're getting close to him," he yelled. "Eleven more licks with the axe and you'll have him!"

"I'm nearer to you, Brer Buzzard," growled Brer Fox, "than I'll be to Brer Rabbit this day. What did you fool me for?"

"Let me alone, Brer Fox," whimpered Mr. Buzzard. "My wife is waiting for me. Brer Rabbit's in there."

"There's a bunch of his fur on that blackberry bush," said Brer Fox, "and that's not the way he came."

Then Mr. Buzzard told Brer Fox the truth, and he said he thought Brer Rabbit was the "lowdownest what's-his-name" that ever he'd met. Whereupon Brer Fox said, "That's neither here nor there, Brer Buzzard. I left you here to watch this hole, and I left Brer Rabbit in there. I come back and I find you at the hole, and Brer Rabbit's not in there. I'm going to make you pay for it! I've been teased to the point where even a little bird will sit on a log and sass me. I'm going to fling you in a brush heap and burn you up!"

"If you fling me on the fire, Brer Fox, I'll fly away," said Mr. Buzzard.

"Well, then, I'll settle your hash right now," growled Brer Fox, and, with that, he grabbed Mr. Buzzard by the tail and was just about to dash him against the ground. Just at that moment the tail feathers came out and Mr. Buzzard sailed off like a balloon, and as he rose, he hollered back, "You gave me a good start, Brer Fox," and Brer Fox sat there and watched him fly out of sight.

Miss Cow Falls Victim to Mr. Rabbit

After Brer Rabbit got out of the hollow tree, he went skipping along home just as sassy as a jaybird. He went galloping along, but he felt mighty tired out and stiff in his joints. He was also dying of thirst, so, when he was almost home and saw old Miss Cow grazing along in a field, he decided to try his hand with her. Brer Rabbit knew that Miss Cow would never give him milk, because she'd refused him more than once, even when Mrs. Rabbit was sick. But never mind: he was determined to try. Brer Rabbit danced up alongside the fence and hollered out, "Howdy, Sis Cow!"

"Why, howdy, Brer Rabbit."

"How do you feel these days, Sis Cow?"

"I'm so-so, Brer Rabbit. How are you doing?"

"Oh, I'm just so-so myself, sort of lingering between half-sick and half-dead," he said.

32

"How your folks, Brer Rabbit?"

"They're just middling, Sis Cow. How's Brer Bull getting on?"

"Sort of middling," said Miss Cow.

"There are some mighty nice persimmons up this tree, Sis Cow," said Brer Rabbit, "and I'd like mighty well to have some of them."

"How you going to get them, Brer Rabbit?" she asked.

"I thought maybe that I might ask you to butt against the tree, and shake some down, Sis Cow," said Brer Rabbit.

Of course, Miss Cow didn't want to make things hard for Brer Rabbit, so she marched up to the persimmon tree and hit it a rap with her horns—blam! Now, those persimmons were green as grass, and not a one dropped. So Miss Cow butted the tree again—blim! But no persimmons dropped. Then, Miss Cow backed off a little further, hoisted her tail on her back, and came against the tree—kerblam! She came so fast and she came so hard that one of her horns went right through the tree, and there she was! She couldn't go forward and she couldn't go backward. This was exactly what Brer Rabbit was waiting for, and he no sooner saw old Miss Cow all fastened up than he jumped up, dancing and prancing.

"Come help me out, Brer Rabbit," mooed Miss Cow.

"I can't climb, Sis Cow," said Brer Rabbit, "but I'll run and tell Brer Bull."

With that, Brer Rabbit put out for home, and it wasn't long before he came back with his wife and all the children, each one carrying a pail. The big ones had big pails, and the little ones had little pails, and they all surrounded old Miss Cow and milked her dry. The old ones milked and the young ones milked, and then, when they'd got enough, Brer Rabbit went up to her and said, "I wish you mighty well, Sis Cow. I figured that, since you'd likely have to camp out all night, I'd better come and milk you so you wouldn't get too full and hurt." Then Brer Rabbit and Mrs. Rabbit and all the little Rabbits ran down the hill with the milk buckets, as pleased as pigs in a peanut patch.

Miss Cow stood there and thought and thought. She tried to break loose, but her horn was jammed in the tree so tight that it took most of the night for her to loosen it. After she got loose, she grazed around, filling her stomach. She figured that, before too long, Brer Rabbit would be hopping along to see how she was getting on, so she laid a trap for him. Just about sunrise, what did old Miss Cow do but march up to the persimmon tree and stick her horn back in the hole. But Brer Rabbit was ahead of her. While she was cropping the grass, he crept back, and when she hitched on to the persimmon tree again, there he was, sitting on the fence corner where she couldn't see him, watching her.

Brer Rabbit said to himself, "Heyo, what's going on now? Hold your horses, Sis Cow, until you hear me coming."

He crept down from the fence and presently, he came—lippity-clippity, clippity-lippity—just sailing down the main road.

"Morning, Sis Cow," said Brer Rabbit. "How are you this morning?"

"Poorly, Brer Rabbit, poorly," said Miss Cow. "I haven't had any rest all

night. I can't pull loose, but if you'll come and catch hold of my tail and pull, Brer Rabbit, I think maybe I can get my horn out." Then Brer Rabbit came up a little closer, but not *too* close.

"I expect I'm near enough, Sis Cow," said he. "I'm a mighty puny man, and I might get trompled. You do the pulling, Sis Cow, and I'll do the grunting."

Then Miss Cow pulled out her horn, and took off after Brer Rabbit at full speed, and down the road they ran, Brer Rabbit with his ears laid back, and Miss Cow with her head down and her tail curled. Brer Rabbit kept on gaining, and, finally, he darted into a brier patch. By the time Miss Cow came along, he had his head sticking out, and his eyes looked as big as china saucers.

"Heyo, Sis Cow! Where you going?" cried Brer Rabbit.

"Howdy there, Brer Big-Eyes," said Miss Cow. "have you seen Brer Rabbit go by?"

"He just this minute passed," said Brer Rabbit, "and he looked mighty sick."

And with that, Miss Cow ran on down the road like the dogs were after her, and Brer Rabbit just lay there in the brier patch, rolling and laughing till his sides hurt. He sure was pleased to laugh: Brer Fox was after him, Brer Buzzard was after him, and now Miss Cow was after him, but they hadn't caught him yet!

Mr. Terrapin Appears on the Scene

One day, after Sis Cow ran past her own shadow trying to catch him, Brer Rabbit decided to drop in on Miss Meadows and the gals. He checked in his looking glass, smoothed his whiskers, and set out.

While cantering along the road, he met his old friend Brer Terrapin, walking along carrying his house on his back like any other turtle. Brer Rabbit stopped, rapped on the roof of Brer Terrapin's house, and asked was he at home. (Brer Terrapin is in the turtle family, so he carries his shell around.) Brer Terrapin allowed that he was, so Brer Rabbit said howdy, and Brer Terrapin responded likewise.

Then Brer Rabbit asked where Brer Terrapin was going, and Brer Terrapin said he wasn't going anywhere, scarcely. So Brer Rabbit invited him to join him in visiting Miss Meadows and the gals, and Brer Terrapin said he didn't mind if he did. They took plenty of time for talking along the way, but, by and by, they got there, and Miss Meadows and the gals did ask them in.

When they got in, Brer Terrapin was so flat-footed that he was too low

37

on the floor, and he wasn't high enough in a chair, so while they were all scrambling around trying to get Brer Terrapin a chair, Brer Rabbit picked him up and put him on the shelf where the water bucket sat. Old Brer Terrapin lay back up there just as proud as he could be.

Of course, they began to talk about Brer Fox. Miss Meadows and the gals said what a great riding horse Brer Fox was, and they made lots of fun of him, laughing and giggling.

Brer Rabbit sat there in the chair smoking his cigar, then cleared his throat, and said, "I'd have ridden him over this morning, ladies, but I rode him so hard yesterday that he went lame in his left foreleg, so I expect I'll have to swap him off yet."

Then Brer Terrapin spoke up: "Well, if you're going to sell him, Brer Rabbit, sell him somewhere way out of this neighborhood. He's been here too long now. Why, only the day before yesterday, Brer Fox passed me on the road, and what do you reckon he said?"

"Mercy, Brer Terrapin," said Miss Meadows, "you don't mean to say he cussed?" And the gals held their fans up before their faces, ashamed even to think about cussing.

"Oh, no, ma'am," answered Brer Terrapin, "he didn't cuss, but he hollered out 'Heyo, Stinky Jim!' "

"Oh, my! Did you hear that, gals? Brer Fox called Brer Terrapin 'Stinky Jim'," she said, and Miss Meadows and the gals wondered how on earth Brer Fox could talk that way about a nice man like Brer Terrapin?

While all this was going on, Brer Fox was standing at the back door with one ear at the keyhole, listening. Eavesdroppers don't hear any good of themselves, and the way Brer Fox was abused that day was a caution.

By and by, Brer Fox stuck his head in the door, and hollered out, "Good evening, folks, I wish you mighty well," and with that, he made a dash for Brer Rabbit! Miss Meadows and the gals hollered and squalled, and Brer Terrapin started to scramble around up on the shelf, and down he came, *blip*, on the back of Brer Fox's head!

This sort of stunned Brer Fox, and when he got his head clear, all he saw was a pot of greens turned over in the fireplace, and a broken chair. Brer

Rabbit was gone, and Brer Terrapin was gone, and Miss Meadows and the gals were gone.

Brer Rabbit had climbed up the chimney—that's what turned the pot of greens over. Brer Terrapin had crept under the bed and got behind the clothes chest, and Miss Meadows and the gals had run out into the yard.

Brer Fox just looked around and felt the back of his head where Brer Terrapin had landed, but he didn't see any sign of Brer Rabbit.

However, the smoke and ashes going up the chimney got the best of Brer Rabbit, and just then, he sneezed—huckychoo!

"Aha!" cried Brer Fox, "you're there, are you? Well, I'm going to smoke you out if it takes a month. You're mine this time!" he said.

Brer Rabbit didn't say a word.

39

"Aren't you coming down?" asked Brer Fox.

Brer Rabbit still stayed mum.

Then Brer Fox went out after some wood. When he came back, he heard Brer Rabbit laughing.

"What you laughing at, Brer Rabbit?"

"Can't tell you, Brer Fox."

"Better tell, Brer Rabbit."

"'Tisn't anything but a box of money somebody left up here in the chink of the chimney," said Brer Rabbit.

"Don't believe you," said Brer Fox.

"Look up and see," said Brer Rabbit, and when Brer Fox looked up, Brer Rabbit spit his eyes full of tobacco juice. Brer Fox made a break for the brook, and Brer Rabbit came down and told the ladies good-bye.

"How did you get rid of him, Brer Rabbit?" asked Miss Meadows.

"Who? Me?" said Brer Rabbit. "Why I just told him that if he didn't go along home and stop playing his pranks on respectable folks, I'd take him out and thrash him."

Mr. Wolf Sets a Trap

Brer Fox felt so bad, and he got so mad about Brer Rabbit, that he didn't know what to do. He felt mighty down-hearted.

One day, while he was going along the road, old Brer Wolf met up with him. When they were done howdying and asking after one another's families, Brer Wolf allowed that it looked like there was something wrong with Brer Fox. Brer Fox said there wasn't, laughed, and made a great to-do because Brer Wolf looked like he suspected something.

But Brer Wolf was pretty smart. He hinted that he'd heard about Brer

41

Rabbit's carryings-on, because the way that Brer Rabbit deceived Brer Fox had gotten to be the talk of the neighborhood. Brer Fox and Brer Wolf kept on talking until, by and by, Brer Wolf said that he had a plan cooked up to trap Brer Rabbit.

Brer Fox asked him how. So, Brer Wolf told him that the way to get the drop on Brer Rabbit was to get him into Brer Fox's house. Brer Fox knew Brer Rabbit of old, and he knew that sort of game was worn to a frazzle, but Brer Wolf talked mightily persuasively.

"How are you going to get him there?" asked Brer Fox.

"Fool him there," said Brer Wolf.

"Who's going to do the fooling?"

"I'll do the fooling," said Brer Wolf, "if you'll do the tricks."

"How you going to do it?"

"You run along home, get on the bed, and pretend you're dead. Don't say anything until Brer Rabbit comes and puts his hands on you," explained Brer Wolf, "and if we don't get him for supper, we're not worth two sticks in the mud."

This looked like a mighty nice game, and Brer Fox agreed. So he ambled off home, and Brer Wolf marched off to Brer Rabbit's house. When he got there, it looked like nobody was at home, but Brer Wolf walked up and knocked on the door— blam! Blam! Nobody came. Then he turned loose and knocked again—blim! blim!

"Who's there?" said Brer Rabbit.

"A friend," said Brer Wolf.

"Too many friends spoil the dinner," said Brer Rabbit. "Which one's this?"

"I bring bad news, Brer Rabbit," said Brer Wolf.

"Bad news is soon told," said Brer Rabbit.

By this time, Brer Rabbit had come to the door, and peeked out cautiously to see who was there.

"Brer Fox died this morning," said Brer Wolf.

"Where's your mourning suit, Brer Wolf?" asked Brer Rabbit.

"Going after it now," said Brer Wolf. "I just called by to bring the news. I went down to Brer Fox's house just a little bit ago, and there I found him stiff."

Then Brer Wolf loped off. Brer Rabbit sat down and scratched his head, and, by and by, he said to himself that he believed he'd just drop around by Brer Fox's house to see how the land lay. No sooner said than done: up he jumped, and out he went. When Brer Rabbit got close to Brer Fox's house all looked lonesome, so he went nearer: nobody stirring. He looked in, and there lay Brer Fox, stretched out on the bed, just as big as life. Brer Rabbit pretended to talk to himself.

"Nobody's round to look after Brer Fox— not even Brer Turkey Buzzard'll come to the funeral," he said. "I hope Brer Fox isn't dead, but I expect he is. Everyone down to Brer Wolf has gone off and left him. It's the busy season with me, but I'll sit up with him. He seems like he's dead, yet he may not be," he said. "When a man goes to see dead folks, dead folks always raise up their behind leg and holler, 'Wahoo!'"

Brer Fox stayed still. So Brer Rabbit talked a little louder. "Mighty funny— Brer Fox looks like he's dead, yet he doesn't act like he's dead. Dead folks hoist their behind leg

and holler, 'Wahoo!' when someone comes to see them," said Brer Rabbit.

Sure enough, Brer Fox lifted up his foot and hollered, "Wahoo!" and Brer Rabbit tore out of the house like the dogs were after him. Brer Wolf was mighty smart, but next time you hear from him, he'll be in trouble.

Mr. Fox Tackles Old Man Terrapin

One day, Brer Fox struck up a conversation with Brer Terrapin right in the middle of the main road. Brer Terrapin had heard him coming, and he thought to himself that he'd keep one eye open, but Brer Fox was monstrous polite, and he opened up the conversation as though he hadn't seen Brer Terrapin since the last rainstorm.

"Hi-ho, Brer Terrapin, where've you been all this time?" said Brer Fox.

"Lounging around, Brer Fox, lounging around," said Brer Terrapin.

"You don't look as good as you used to, Brer Terrapin," said Brer Fox.

"Lounging around and suffering," said Brer Terrapin.

Then the talk went on like this:

"What ails you, Brer Terrapin? Your eye looks mighty red," said Brer Fox.

"Lord, Brer Fox, you don't know what trouble is. You haven't been lounging around and suffering."

"Both your eyes look red, and you look like you're mighty weak, Brer Terrapin."

"Lord, Brer Fox, you don't know what trouble is."

"What ails you now, Brer Terrapin?"

"Took a walk the other day, and a man came along and set the field on fire. Lord, Brer Fox, you don't know what trouble is," said Brer Terrapin.

"How did you get out of the fire, Brer Terrapin?"

"Sat and took it, Brer Fox. Sat and took it, and the smoke got in my eyes, and the fire scorched my back."

"It burned your tail off, too," said Brer Fox.

"Oh, no, here's my tail, Brer Fox," said Brer Terrapin, and with that, he uncurled his tail from under his shell. And no sooner did he do that, than Brer Fox grabbed it, and hollered out: "Oh yes, Brer Terrapin! Oh yes! So you're the one who hit me on the head at Miss Meadows's, are you? Well, I'm going to do you in."

Brer Terrapin begged and begged, but it was no use. Brer Fox had been fooled so much that he looked as though he was determined to let Brer Terrapin have it. Then Brer Terrapin begged Brer Fox not to drown him, but Brer Fox wasn't making any promises, and then he begged Brer Fox to burn him, because he was used to fire, but Brer Fox said nothing. By and by, Brer Fox dragged Brer Terrapin off a little way below the spring house, and ducked him under the water.

Then Brer Terrapin began to holler, "Turn loose that stump root and catch hold of me—turn loose that stump root and catch hold of me!"

Brer Fox hollered back, "I haven't got hold of a stump root, I've got hold of you." Brer Terrapin kept on hollering, "Catch hold of me—I'm drowning—I'm drowning—turn loose the stump root and catch hold of me."

Sure enough, Brer Fox turned loose the tail, and Brer Terrapin went down to the bottom—kerblunkity-blink.

Old man Terrapin was glad to be at home—kerblinkity-blunk!

Mr. Fox and the Deceitful Frogs

When Brer Fox turned Brer Terrapin loose in the brook, Brer Terrapin said, "Idoom-er-ker-kum-mer-ker!" Brer Terrapin was at the bottom of the pond, and so he talked in bubbles—I doom-er-ker-kum-mer-ker! Brer Fox said nothing, but Brer Bull-Frog, sitting on the bank, heard Brer Terrapin and he hollered back, "Jug-er-rum-kum-dum! Jug-er-rum-kum-dum!"

Then another Frog hollered out, "Knee-deep! Knee-deep!"

So old Brer Bull-Frog hollered back, "Don't you-be-lieve-'im! Don't-you-be-lieve-'im!"

Then the bubbles came up from Brer Terrapin, "I-doom-er-ker-kum-mer-ker!"

And another Frog sang out, "Wade in! Wade in!"

Then old Brer Bull-Frog talked through his hoarse-ness, "There-you'll-find-your-brother! There-you'll-find-your-brother!"

48

Sure enough, Brer Fox looked over the bank, and there was another Fox looking at him out of the water. He reached out to shake hands and in he went, heels over head, and Brer Terrapin bubbled out, "I-doom-er-ker-kum-mer-ker!"

Brer Fox wasn't exactly drowned. He managed to scramble out, just before Brer Mud Turtle got his tail and dragged him off for dinner.

Mr. Fox Goes A-Hunting, But Mr. Rabbit Bags the Game

B rer Fox and Brer Rabbit were always running into one another. Lots of times, Brer Fox could have nabbed Brer Rabbit, but every time he got the chance, he would think of the number of times he'd been tricked, and he would let Brer Rabbit alone. By and by, they began to get familiar with

one another like the old days, and it got so Brer Fox would call on Brer Rabbit, and they'd sit up and smoke their pipes like no harsh feelings had ever been between them.

Then one day, Brer Fox came along all rigged out, and asked Brer Rabbit to go hunting with him, but Brer Rabbit felt sort of lazy, and he told Brer Fox that he had some other fish to fry. Brer Fox felt mighty sorry, but he said he believed he'd try his hand anyhow, and off he went. He was gone all day, and he had a monstrous streak of luck, bagging a heap of game. By and by, toward the end of the evening, Brer Rabbit stretched himself and decided it was almost time for Brer Fox to get home. He climbed up on a stump to see if he could hear Brer Fox coming. Pretty soon, there was Brer Fox coming through the woods, singing his head off. Brer Rabbit leaped off the stump and lay down in the road as if he were dead.

Brer Fox came along and saw him lying there. He turned him over to examine him, and said, "This here Rabbit's dead, and he looks like he's been dead a long time. He's dead, but he's mighty fat. He's the fattest rabbit I've ever seen, but he's been dead too long. I'm afraid to take him home."

Brer Rabbit said nothing. Brer Fox licked his chops, but he went on and left Brer Rabbit lying in the road. As soon as he was out of sight, Brer Rabbit jumped up, ran around through the woods, and got ahead of Brer Fox again. Brer Fox came up, and there lay Brer Rabbit, looking cold and stiff.

50

Brer Fox looked at Brer Rabbit and thought a while. Then he unslung his game bag, and said to himself, "These here rabbits are going to waste. I'll just leave my game here, and I'll go back and get that other rabbit, then I'll make folks believe that I'm the best hunter in Huntsville!"

And with that, he dropped his game bag and loped back up the road after the other rabbit. Of course, when he got out of sight, old Brer Rabbit snatched up Brer Fox's game and ran for home. Next time he saw Brer Fox, he hollered out, "What did you kill the other day, Brer Fox?"

Then Brer Fox combed his flank with his tongue, sheepishly, and hollered back, "I caught a handful of hard sense, Brer Rabbit."

Then old Brer Rabbit, he laughed and said, "If I'd known you were after that, Brer Fox, I'd a loaned you some of mine!"

Mr. Rabbit Is a Good Fisherman

Brer Rabbit and Brer Fox were like some children: both of them were always after one another, pranking and pestering around, but now, Brer Rabbit had some peace, because Brer Fox had gotten skittish about going after him.

One day, Brer Rabbit, Brer Fox, Brer Raccoon, Brer Bear, and a whole lot of their neighbors were clearing new ground to plant a corn patch. Pretty soon, the sun began to get hot and Brer Rabbit got tired, but he didn't let on because he was afraid the rest of them would call him lazy. So he kept toting off trash and piling up brush, until, by and by, he hollered out that he'd gotten a brier in his hand. Then he slipped off to hunt for a cool place to rest. After a while, he came across a well with a bucket hanging in it.

"That looks cool," said Brer Rabbit to himself, "and cool I expect it is. I'll just get in there and take a nap," and with that, in he jumped, and he'd no sooner jumped into the bucket than the bucket began to go down.

And right then, there's been no more scared a beast since the world began than Brer Rabbit—he almost trembled into pieces. He knew where he came from, but not where he was going. Suddenly, he felt the bucket hit the water, and there it sat. He kept mighty still, because he didn't know what was going to happen next. He just lay there and shook and shivered.

Brer Fox always had one eye on Brer Rabbit, and when he slipped off from the new patch, Brer Fox snuck after him. He knew Brer Rabbit was up to something, so he crept after him to watch what he would do. Brer Fox saw Brer Rabbit come to the well and stop, and then he saw him jump into the bucket, and then, lo and behold, he saw him go down out of sight. Brer Fox was the most astonished Fox that you ever laid eyes on. He sat there in

the bushes and thought and thought, but he couldn't make head or tail of this kind of business.

"Well, if this doesn't beat anything I've ever seen!" he said to himself. "I bet that right down there in that well, Brer Rabbit keeps his money hidden, and if it's not that, then he's gone and discovered a gold mine, and if it's not that, then I'm going to see what's in there!"

Brer Fox crept up a little nearer and listened, but he heard no fuss. He kept on getting nearer, and still heard nothing. By and by, he got up close and peeped down, but he saw nothing and he heard nothing. All this time, Brer Rabbit was absolutely scared out of his skin, afraid to move because the bucket might keel over and spill him out into the water.

While he said his prayers over like a train of railroad cars running, old Brer Fox hollered out, "Heyo, Brer Rabbit! Who you visiting down there?"

"Who? Me? Oh, I'm just fishing, Brer Fox," said Brer Rabbit. "I just said to myself that I'd surprise you all with a mess of fish for dinner, and so here I am, and there's the fish. I'm fishing for suckers, Brer Fox."

"Are there many of them down there, Brer Rabbit?" asked Brer Fox.

"Lots of them, Brer Fox, scores and scores of them. The water is alive with them. Come down and help me haul them in, Brer Fox," said Brer Rabbit.

"How I'm going to get down, Brer Rabbit?"

"Jump in the other bucket, Brer Fox. It'll fetch you down all safe and sound."

Brer Rabbit talked so happy and talked so sweet that Brer Fox jumped into the other bucket and, as he went down, of course, his weight pulled Brer Rabbit up. When they passed one another half way, Brer Rabbit sang out,

"Good-by, Brer Fox, take care of your clothes,
For this is the way the world goes;
Some go up and some go down.
You'll get to the bottom all safe and sound."

When Brer Rabbit got out, he galloped off and told the folks that Brer Fox was down in the well muddying up the drinking water, and then he galloped back to the well, and hollered down to Brer Fox,

"Here comes a man with a great big gun!
When he hauls you up, you jump and run."

In just about half an hour, both of them were back on the new ground working like they'd never heard of a well, except that every now and then, Brer Rabbit would burst out in a laugh, and old Brer Fox could only pretend to smile back.

Mr. Rabbit Nibbles Up the Butter

The animals of the neighborhood kept getting more and more friendly with one another until, by and by, it wasn't long before Brer Rabbit and Brer Fox and Brer Possum got to storing their provisions together in the same shanty. One day, the roof began to leak, and so Brer Rabbit, Brer Fox, and Brer Possum got together to see if they could patch it up. They had a big day's work ahead of them, so they brought their dinner with them. They put the food in one pile, and put the butter that Brer Fox had brought in the springhouse to keep cool. Then they went to work, and it wasn't long before Brer Rabbit's stomach began to growl and pester him. That butter of Brer Fox's sat heavy on his mind, and his mouth watered every time he thought about it. Presently, he said to himself that he had to have a nip at that butter, so he made his plans.

First thing you know, Brer Rabbit raised his head quick and flung his ears forward and hollered out, "Here I am. What you want with me?" and off he ran like something was after him.

He ran until he was sure nobody was following him, then into the springhouse he bounced, and there he stayed until he got a bite of butter. Then he sauntered on back and to work.

"Where you been?" asked Brer Fox.

"I heard my children calling me," said Brer Rabbit, "and I had to go see what they wanted. Mrs. Rabbit suddenly got mighty sick."

They worked on until, by and by, the butter tasted so good that old Brer Rabbit wanted some more. Then he raised up his head and hollered out, "Heyo! Hold on! I'm a-coming!" and off he went.

This time he stayed quite a long while, and when he got back, Brer Fox asked him where he'd been.

"I've been to see my wife, and she's feeling worse," said Brer Rabbit.

Pretty soon, Brer Rabbit heard the butter calling him again, and off he went. This time, he got the butter out so neatly that he could see himself in

56

the bottom of the bucket. He scraped
it clean and licked it dry, and then
went back to work looking as if
he'd been caught by the hunters.
"How's your wife this time?"
asked Brer Fox.

"I'm obliged to you, Brer Fox,"
said Brer Rabbit, "but I'm afraid
she's gone by now," and that made
Brer Fox and Brer Possum feel sorry
for him.

Finally, when dinner time came, they all got out the vittles, but Brer
Rabbit kept on looking lonesome, and Brer Fox and Brer Possum rustled
around to see if they couldn't make Brer Rabbit feel better. By and by, Brer
Fox said, "Brer Possum, you run down to the spring and fetch the butter,
and I'll run around here and set the table."

Brer Possum loped off after the butter and quickly came loping back
with his ears a-trembling and his tongue hanging out. Brer Fox hollered
out, "What's the matter now, Brer Possum?"

"You all better run here, folks," said Brer Possum. "The last drop of that
butter's all gone!"

"Where's it gone?" asked Brer Fox.

"Looks like it dried up," replied Brer Possum.

Then Brer Rabbit, looking solemn, said "I expect that butter melted in
somebody's mouth."

Then, they went down to the spring with Brer Possum and sure enough,
the butter was all gone. While they were disputing this and wondering,
Brer Rabbit said he saw tracks all around there, and he pointed out that, if
they would all go to sleep, he could catch the fellow who stole the butter.
They all lay down, and Brer Fox and Brer Possum soon dropped off to sleep.
But Brer Rabbit stayed awake, and when the time came he got up quietly
and smeared Brer Possum's mouth with the butter on his paws. Then he
ran off and nibbled up the best of the dinner that they'd left out, came back,

and woke Brer Fox, and showed him the butter on Brer Possum's mouth. They woke up Brer Possum and told him about it, but, of course, Brer Possum denied it to the last.

Now, Brer Fox was a kind of lawyer, so he argued that Brer Possum was the first one at the butter, and the first one to miss it, and more than that, there were the signs on his mouth. Brer Possum saw that he was jammed in a corner, and so he said that the way to catch the one that stole the butter was to build a big brush heap, set it afire, and all hands try to jump over it. The one that had the most trouble jumping over would be the fellow that stole the butter.

Brer Rabbit and Brer Fox both agreed. So they whirled in and built the brush heap, they built it high and wide, and then they lit it up. When it got to blazing up good, Brer Rabbit took the first turn. He stepped back, looked around and giggled, and over he went, just like a bird flying. Then came Brer Fox. He got back a little further, spit on his hands, lit out and made the jump, and he came so near getting into the fire that the under side of his tail caught fire. Next time you see a fox, look right close and see if the underside of his tail's not white. All foxes bear the scar of that brush heap to this day—they are marked, for all time.

When it came time for Brer Possum to jump, he got so scared he flopped over flat on his back in the grass the way possums do, and lay so still, Brer Rabbit and Brer Fox thought he was dead. They both shed tears for him over the dying fire before they went off home. And Brer Possum didn't even take a breath until they'd gone.

Mr. Rabbit Finds His Match at Last

One day, when Brer Rabbit was going lippity-clippiting down the road, he met up with old Brer Terrapin, and after they had passed the time of day for a while, Brer Rabbit said he was much obliged to Brer Terrapin for the hand he took in the rumpus that other day down at Miss Meadows's.

Brer Terrapin said that Brer Fox ran mighty fast that day, but that if he'd run after him instead of Brer Rabbit he'd have caught him. Brer Rabbit said he could have caught him himself, but he didn't want to leave the ladies.

59

They kept on talking till they got to disputing about which was the swiftest. Brer Rabbit said he could outrun Brer Terrapin, and Brer Terrapin vowed he could outrun Brer Rabbit. Up and down they had it, until, first news you know, Brer Terrapin said he had a fifty-dollar bill in the chink of the chimney at home, and that bill told him he could beat Brer Rabbit in a fair race. Then Brer Rabbit said he had a fifty-dollar bill that said he could leave Brer Terrapin so far behind that he could sow barley as he went along and it would be ripe enough to cut by the time Brer Terrapin passed that way.

Anyhow, they made the bet and put up the money, and old Brer Turkey Buzzard was summoned to be the judge and the stakeholder. Miss Meadows and the gals and most all the neighbors got wind of the fun, and when the day was set, they made plans to be on hand.

It wasn't long before all the arrangements were made. The race was five miles long, the ground was measured off, and at the end of every mile, a milepost was set up. Brer Rabbit was to run down the main road, but Brer Terrapin said he'd gallop through the woods. Folks told him he could get along faster in the road, but old Brer Terrapin knew what he was doing.

60

Brer Rabbit trained every day, and he skipped over the ground just as gaily as a June cricket, but old Brer Terrapin just lay low in the swamp. He had a wife and three children, old Brer Terrapin did, and they were all the very spit and image of the old man. Everybody who wanted to tell one from the other had to take a spy glass, and even then they were liable to get fooled.

That's the way matters stood until the day of the race, and on that day, old Brer Terrapin, his wife, and his three children got up before sunrise and went to the race course. Mrs. Terrapin took her stand near the starting post, the children near each of the mileposts, and then old Brer Terrapin took his position near the finish line. By and by, everybody came: Judge Buzzard, Miss Meadows and the gals, and then Brer Rabbit, with ribbons tied around his neck and streaming from his ears. The spectators all went to the end of the track where they could see the finish of the race.

When the time came, Judge Buzzard strutted around and pulled out his watch, and hollered out, "Gents, are you ready?"

Brer Rabbit said "Yes," and old Mrs. Terrapin hollered "Go!" from the edge of the woods. Brer Rabbit lit out on the race, and old Mrs. Terrapin headed for home. Judge Buzzard rose and skimmed along to see that the

race was run fair. When Brer Rabbit got to the first milepost, one of the Terrapin children crawled out of the woods and made for the post. Brer Rabbit hollered out, "Where are you, Brer Terrapin?"

"Here I come a-bulging," said the Terrapin.

Brer Rabbit was so glad he was ahead that he ran harder than ever, while the Terrapin made for home. When Brer Rabbit came to the next post, another Terrapin crawled out of the woods.

"Where are you, Brer Terrapin?" said Brer Rabbit.

"Here I come a-boiling," called the Terrapin.

Brer Rabbit lit out and came to the third post, and there was the Terrapin. Then he came to the next, and there was the Terrapin. Then he had one more mile to run, and he felt like he was losing his breath. Finally, old Brer Terrapin looked down the road and saw Judge Buzzard sailing along and he knew it was time for him to be up and moving. So he scrambled out of the woods, rolled across the ditch, shuffled through the crowd of folks and got to the final milepost and crawled behind it.

By and by, first thing you know, there came Brer Rabbit. He looked around, but he didn't see Brer Terrapin, and so he squalled out, "Gimme the money, Brer Buzzard! Gimme the money!"

Miss Meadows and the gals shouted and laughed fit to kill themselves, and old Brer Terrapin just raised up from behind the post and said, "If you'll give me time to catch my breath, ladies and gents, one and all, I expect I'll take that money myself." And sure enough, Brer Terrapin tied the purse around his neck and skedaddled off home.

A Lesson for Mr. Jack Sparrow

One day, after he'd been fooled by old Brer Terrapin, Brer Rabbit was sitting in the woods deciding how he was going to get even with the world. He felt mighty lonesome, and he felt mighty mad. He sat there by himself and thought and thought, until, suddenly, he jumped up and yelled, "Well, doggone my cats if I can't run rings around old Brer Fox, and I'm going to do it. I'll show Miss Meadows and the gals that I'm the boss of Brer Fox!"

Jack Sparrow, up in the tree, heard Brer Rabbit and sang out, "I'm going to tell Brer Fox! I'm going to tell Brer Fox! Chick-a-biddy-wind-a-blowing-acorns-falling! I'm going to tell Brer Fox!"

This kind of terrified Brer Rabbit, and he scarcely knew what to do. But, by and by, he realized that the one who saw Brer Fox first was bound to have the best of it, and he hopped off towards home. He hadn't gone far when whom should he meet but Brer Fox, so right away he said, "What's this between you and me, Brer Fox? I hear tell you're going to send me to destruction, nab my family, and destroy my shanty."

That made Brer Fox mighty mad. "Who's been telling you all this?" he shouted.

Brer Rabbit pretended he didn't want

63

to tell, but Brer Fox insisted and insisted, till at last Brer Rabbit told him that he heard Jack Sparrow say all this.

"Of course," said Brer Rabbit, "when Brer Jack Sparrow told me that, I jumped up and used some language which I'm mighty glad no children were around to hear."

Brer Fox sort of yawned, then said he expected he'd better be sauntering on. But Brer Fox hadn't sauntered far before Jack Sparrow flipped down on a bush by the side of the road, and sang out, "Brer Fox! Oh, Brer Fox!—Brer Fox!"

Brer Fox just sort of cantered along and made as if he didn't hear him. So Jack Sparrow sang out again, "Brer Fox! Oh, Brer Fox! Hold on, Brer Fox! I've got some news for you. Wait, Brer Fox! It'll surprise you no end!"

Brer Fox pretended he couldn't see Jack Sparrow or hear him, but he lay down by the road, and stretched himself out as if he was going to take a nap. The tattling Jack Sparrow flew along, calling Brer Fox, but Brer Fox didn't answer. Then little Jack Sparrow hopped down on the ground and fluttered around in the leaves. This attracted Brer Fox's attention. He looked at the tattling bird, and the bird kept on calling, "I got something to tell you, Brer Fox."

"Get on my tail, little Jack Sparrow," said Brer Fox, "because I'm deaf in one ear, and I can't hear out of the other. Get on my tail."

So the little bird hopped onto Brer Fox's tail.

"Get on my back, little Jack Sparrow. I'm deaf in one ear, and I can't hear out of the other."

The little bird hopped on his back.

"Hop on my tooth, little Jack Sparrow. I'm deaf in one ear, and can't hear out of the other."

The tattling little bird started to hop onto Brer Fox's tooth when, all of a sudden, "*Kerchoof!*"—Brer Fox sneezed. He sneezed so hard he blew Jack Sparrow up in the air, and about that time Jack Sparrow decided to fly as fast as he could to the next town, in the next county, on the other side of the mountain, where Brer Fox could never find him and eat him up. And he didn't tattle on anyone for three whole weeks after that.

How Mr. Rabbit Saved His Cow

One day, Brer Wolf was coming home from a fishing frolic. He sauntered along the road with a string of fish across his shoulder, when suddenly, Miss Partridge hopped out of the bushes and fluttered down next to Brer Wolf's nose. Brer Wolf told himself that old Miss Partridge was trying to lead him away from her nest, and so he put his fish down and hid in the bushes where he'd first seen Miss Partridge. About that time, Brer Rabbit happened along. There were Brer Wolf's fish, there was Brer Rabbit, and when that's the case, what do you expect Brer Rabbit's going to do? Those fish didn't stay where Brer Wolf put them, that's for sure, and when Brer Wolf came back, they were gone.

Brer Wolf sat down and scratched his head and thought and thought, and it finally occured to him that Brer Rabbit had been along there. Brer Wolf set out for Brer Rabbit's house, and when he got there, he hailed him, but Brer Rabbit said he didn't know anything at all about the fish. Brer Wolf

said he had to believe Brer Rabbit had those fish. Brer Rabbit said that, if Brer Wolf thought he'd taken the fish, he could take the Rabbit family's best cow. Brer Wolf took Brer Rabbit at his word, and

started out to the pasture to get it.

Brer Rabbit hated to lose this cow, so he made a plan. Brer Wolf had got caught by hunters in the past and was mighty scared of them, so Brer Rabbit hollered out, "Hold up, there, Brer Wolf! I hear the hunters coming! You'll have to run and hide until they pass. I'll stay here and get the cow for you and have it ready when you get back."

As soon as Brer Wolf heard talk of the hunters, he scrambled off into the underbrush like he'd been shot out of a gun. And as soon as he'd gone, Brer Rabbit whirled around and grabbed his old fly swatter made out of a cow's tail, from a nail on the wall. He stuck the end of it into the ground, then he squalled out for Brer Wolf, "Run here, Brer Wolf! Run here! The hunters are gone, and your cow is sinking into the ground. Run here!"

When old Brer Wolf got there—and he came scooting—there was Brer Rabbit pretending to hold onto the tail to keep the cow from sinking into the ground. Brer Wolf caught hold, and they began to pull, and up came the tail without the cow. Then Brer Rabbit laughed to himself and said, "There! The tail's pulled out and the cow's gone!"

But Brer Wolf wasn't about to give up that easy. He got a spade, and a pickax and a shovel, and he dug and dug for that cow until digging was past all endurance. Brer Rabbit sat up there on his front porch and smoked his cigar. Every time old Brer Wolf stuck the pickax into the clay, Brer Rabbit winked at his children. "He diggy-diggy-digs, but no cow's there! He diggy-diggy-digs, but no cow's there!"

True enough—because all this time, the cow was up in the far pasture, eating the grass and flicking flies off her flanks with her long, strong tail. And all Brer Wolf had was an old fly swatter.

Mr. Rabbit Meets His Match Again

There was someone else who played as sharp as Brer Rabbit. In the old days, animals acted the same as people: they went into farming, ran small businesses, had parties, and went to church when the weather was nice. Where there was one smart person, there was often another. If nobody had ever gotten the best of Brer Rabbit, the neighbors would have taken him for a witch, and in those times they burned witches before you could blink your eyelids.

One time, Brer Rabbit and old Brer Buzzard decided they'd go shares and farm together. It was a mighty good year, and the crops turned out monstrous well, but, by and by, when the time came for division, it turned out that old Brer Buzzard got nothing. The crop was all gone, and there was nothing there to show for it. Brer Rabbit pretended he was in a worse fix than Brer Buzzard, and he moped around like he was afraid he wouldn't have a bite to eat all winter.

Brer Buzzard didn't say anything, but he did do a lot of thinking, and one day he came along and yelled at Brer Rabbit that he'd found a rich gold mine just across the river.

"You come along with me, Brer Rabbit," said Brer Turkey Buzzard. "I'll scratch and you can grab, and, between the two of us, we'll make short work of that gold mine."

Brer Rabbit certainly was up for the job, but he wondered how he was going to get across the water, because every time he got his feet wet, he caught cold. He asked Brer Buzzard what to do, and Brer Buzzard promised to carry Brer Rabbit across. In fact, right then and there, old Brer Buzzard squatted down and spread his wings, Brer Rabbit climbed on, and up they rose.

They rose, and when they lit, they lit in the top of the highest pine tree that was growing on an island in the middle of the river, with the deep water running all around.

As soon as they had landed, Brer Rabbit realized what Brer Buzzard was plotting and by the time the old bird had got himself balanced on a limb, Brer Rabbit said, "While we're resting here, Brer Buzzard, and since you've been so good, I got something to tell you. I've got a gold mine of my own, one that I dug myself, and I expect we better go back to mine it before we bother with another one."

Then Brer Buzzard laughed till his big black wings shook, and Brer Rabbit sang out, "Hold on, Brer Buzzard! Don't flap your wings when you laugh, because, if you do, something will drop from up here, and my gold mine won't do you any good, and neither will yours do me any good!"

However, before Brer Buzzard would leave, Brer Rabbit had to tell him all about the crop, and he had to promise to divide it fair and square. Then Brer Buzzard carried him back, and Brer Rabbit was weak in the knees for a month afterwards.

A Story About the Little Rabbits

Find them where you will and when you may, good children always get taken care of. For instance, there were Brer Rabbit's children: they minded their daddy and mommy from day's beginning to day's end. When old man Rabbit said "Scoot," they scooted, and when old Mrs. Rabbit said "Scat," they scatted. And they kept their clothes clean, and they had no smut on their noses, either.

71

They were good children, and if they hadn't been, there was one time when there wouldn't have been any little rabbits—nary a one.

That was the time when Brer Fox dropped in at Brer Rabbit's house and found nobody there but the little Rabbits. Brer Rabbit

was off somewhere raiding a collard patch, and Mrs. Rabbit was at a quilting bee in the neighborhood, and, while the little Rabbits were playing hide-and-seek, in dropped Brer Fox. The little Rabbits were so fat that they fairly made his mouth water, but he remembered how clever Brer Rabbit was, so he was scared to gobble them up unless he had some excuse. The little Rabbits were mighty skittish, and they sort of huddled themselves up together and watched Brer Fox's motions. Brer Fox sat there figuring out what sort of excuse he was going to make up. By and by, he noticed a great big stalk of sugar cane standing up in the corner, and he cleared his throat and said arrogantly, "Hey! You young Rabs there, sail around here and break me off a piece of that sweeting-tree," and then he coughed.

The little Rabbits got out the sugar cane, and they wrestled with it, and sweated over it, but it was no use: they couldn't break it. Brer Fox pretended he wasn't watching, but he kept on hollering, "Hurry up there, Rabs! I'm waiting for you."

And the little Rabbits hustled 'round and wrestled with it some more, but they still couldn't break it. Just then, they heard a little bird singing on top of the house, and the song that the little bird sang was this:

> "Take your teeth and gnaw it,
> Take your teeth and saw it,
> Saw it and yoke it,
> And then you can broke it."

Then the little Rabbits felt mighty glad and they gnawed the cane almost before old Brer Fox could get his legs uncrossed, and when they carried him the cane, Brer Fox sat there and thought how to make some other excuse for nabbing one of them.

By and by, he stood up and got down the flour sifter that was hanging on the wall, and hollered out, "Come here, Rabs! Take this sifter and run down to the spring and fetch me some fresh water."

The little Rabbits ran down to the spring, and tried to dip up the water with the sifter, but, of course, it all ran out and it kept on running out until the little Rabbits sat down and began to cry. Then the little bird sitting up in the tree began to sing, and this was the song he sang:

> "Sifter holds water same as a tray,
> If you fill it with moss and daub it with clay;
> The fox will get madder the longer you stay—
> Fill it with moss and daub it with clay."

Up they jumped, the little Rabbits did, and they fixed the sifter so it wouldn't leak, and then they carried the water to old Brer Fox. So Brer Fox got mighty mad, and pointed out a great stick of wood, and told the little Rabbits to put it on the fire. The little chaps got around the wood, and they tried so hard to lift it that their eyes almost popped out of their heads, but the wood didn't budge. They they heard the little bird singing again, and this is the song he sang:

> "Spit in your hands and tug it and toll it,
> And get behind it, and push it, and pole it;
> Spit in your hands and rear back and roll it."

And just about the time they got the wood on the fire, their daddy came skipping in and the little bird flew away. Brer Fox saw his game was up and it wasn't long before he made his excuses and started to go.

"You better stay and have a snack with me, Brer Fox," said Brer Rabbit. "I haven't had many visitors lately, and I'm getting so I feel right lonesome these long nights."

But Brer Fox buttoned up his coat collar tight and just started for home.

Mr. Rabbit and Mr. Bear

There came a season when Brer Fox said to himself that he better get busy and plant a peanut patch, and in those days, it was touch and go. The words weren't more than out of his mouth before the ground was broken up and the peanuts were planted. Old Brer Rabbit sat and watched Brer Fox at work, then he shut one eye and sang to his children:

> "Ti-yi Tungalee!
> I eat the pea, I pick the pea.
> It grows in the ground, it grows so free;
> Ti-yi the peanut pea."

Sure enough, when the peanuts began to ripen, every time Brer Fox went down to his peanut patch, he found somebody'd been grabbling among the vines and he got mighty mad. He sort of knew who the somebody was, but old Brer Rabbit covered his tracks so cute that Brer Fox didn't know how to catch him.

One day, Brer Fox took a walk all around the peanut patch, and it wasn't long before he found a crack in the fence where the rail had been rubbed smooth, and right there he set a trap. He bent down a hickory sapling growing in the corner of the fence, tied one end of rope to the top of the tree, and on the other end he made a loop knot. Then he fastened it so that it would catch anyone going through the crack.

The next morning, when old Brer Rabbit came slipping along and crept through the crack in the fence, the loop knot caught him behind the forelegs, the sapling flew up, and there he was, 'twixt the heavens and the earth. There he swung and he feared he was going to fall, and he also feared he wasn't going to fall. While he was fixing up a tale for Brer Fox, he heard

76

a lumbering on down the road, and presently here came old Brer Bear ambling along from where he'd been raiding a bee tree.

Brer Rabbit hailed him, "Howdy, Brer Bear!"

Brer Bear looked around and, by and by, he saw Brer Rabbit swinging from the sapling, and he hollered out, "Heyo, Brer Rabbit! How are you this morning?"

"Much obliged. I'm middling, Brer Bear."

Then Brer Bear asked Brer Rabbit what was he doing up there in the air, and Brer Rabbit said he was making a dollar a minute. Brer Bear asked how. Brer Rabbit said he was keeping the crows out of Brer Fox's peanut patch, and then he asked Brer Bear if he didn't want to make a dollar a minute too, because he'd got a big family of children to take care of and he'd make such a nice scarecrow. Brer Bear allowed that he'd take the job, and so Brer Rabbit showed him how to bend down the sapling and it wasn't long before Brer Bear was swinging up there in Brer Rabbit's place.

Then Brer Rabbit set out for Brer Fox's house, and when he got there he

sang out, "Brer Fox! Oh, Brer Fox! Come out here, Brer Fox, and I'll show you who's been stealing your peanuts."

Brer Fox grabbed up his walking stick, and both of them went running back down to the peanut patch, and when they got there, sure enough, there was old Brer Bear.

"Oh, yes! You're caught, aren't you?" says Brer Fox, and before Brer Bear could explain, Brer Rabbit jumped up and down and hollered out, "Give him what-for, Brer Fox, give him what-for," and Brer Fox drew back and yelled, "Why'd you steal my peanuts? Why?" And every time Brer Bear tried to explain, Brer Fox yelled at him and hit him with a stick.

While all this was going on, Brer Rabbit slipped off, got in a mud hole and left just his eyes sticking out, because he knew that Brer Bear would be coming after him.

Sure enough, by and by, Brer Bear came down the road, and when the got to the mud hole, he said, "Howdy, Brer Frog, did you see Brer Rabbit go by here?"

"He's just gone by," said Brer Frog, and old man Bear took off down the road like a scared mule, while Brer Rabbit came out and dried himself in the sun, and then went home to his family the same as any other day.

Mr. Bear Catches Old Mr. Bullfrog

Brer Bear decided that old Brer Bullfrog was the man who fooled him, and he said he'd catch up with him if it was a year afterwards. But it wasn't a year, and it wasn't a month, and more than that, it wasn't scarcely a week, when, one day, Brer Bear was going home from taking a bee tree, and, lo and behold, who should he see but old Brer Bullfrog sitting out on the edge of the mud puddle fast asleep! Brer Bear dropped his axe, crept up, reached out with his paw, and scooped Brer Bullfrog in. When Brer Bear got his clampers on him, he sat down and talked to him.

"Howdy, Brer Bullfrog, howdy! And how's your family? I hope they're well, Brer Bullfrog, because this day you got some business with me that'll last you a mighty long time."

Brer Bullfrog didn't know what to say. He didn't know what was up and he didn't say a thing. Old Brer Bear kept talking:

"You're the man who fooled me about Brer Rabbit the other day. You had your fun, Brer Bullfrog, and now I'll get mine."

80

Then Brer Bullfrog began to get scared, and said, "What have I been doing, Brer Bear? How have I been fooling you?"

Then Brer Bear laughed, and made like he didn't know, but he kept on talking. "Oh, no, Brer Bullfrog! You're not the one who stuck your head up out of the water and told me Brer Rabbit's gone on by. Oh, no! You're not the one: I'm bound you're not. About that time, you were at home with your family, where you always are. I don't know where you were, but I know where you are now, Brer Bullfrog, and it's just you and me here. After the sun goes down this day, you won't fool any more folks going along this road."

Of course, Brer Bullfrog didn't know what Brer Bear was driving at, but he knew something had to be done, and mighty soon, too, because Brer Bear began to snap his jaws together and foam at the mouth.

Brer Bullfrog hollered out, "Oh, pray, Brer Bear! Let me off this time, and I won't ever do that again. Oh, pray, Brer Bear, do let me off this time, and I'll show you the fattest bee tree in the woods."

Old Brer Bear chomped his teeth and foamed at the mouth. Brer Bullfrog squalled louder, "Oh pray, Brer Bear! I won't ever do it again! Oh, pray, Brer Bear! Let me off this time!"

But old Brer Bear said he was going to make away with him, and then he sat and tried to figure out how in this wide world he could do it. He knew he couldn't drown him, and he had no fire to burn him, so he got mighty bothered.

By and by, old Brer Bullfrog stopped his crying and his boo-hooing, and he said, "If you're going to kill me, Brer Bear, carry me to that big flat rock out there on the edge of the millpond, where I can see my family, and after I see them, then you can take your axe and squash me."

This sounded so fair and square that Brer Bear agreed, and he took Brer Bullfrog by one of his hind legs, slung his axe on his shoulder, and off he went for the big flat rock. When he got there, he put Brer Bullfrog down on the rock, and Brer Bullfrog pretended to look around for his folks. Then Brer Bear drew a long breath and picked up his axe. He spat in his hands and drew back and came down on the rock—*pow!*

81

But he didn't kill the frog. Between the time Brer Bear raised up his axe and when he came down with it, old Brer Bullfrog leapt up and dove down into the millpond, kerblink-kerblunk! And when he rose, way out in the pond, he rose singing, and this is the song he sang:

"Ingle-go-jang, my joy, my joy—
Ingle-go-jang, my joy!
I'm right at home, my joy, my joy—
Ingle-go-jang, my joy!"

That sounds like a mighty strange song now, but it wasn't strange in those days, and it wouldn't be strange now if folks knew as much about the Bullfrog language as they used to.

How Mr. Rabbit Lost His Fine Bushy Tail

One time, Brer Rabbit was going along down the road shaking his big bushy tail, feeling just as scrumptious as a blue jay with a fresh bug. Who should he run across but old Brer Fox ambling along with a big string of fish!

When they'd passed the time of day for a while, Brer Rabbit asked Brer Fox where he got that nice string of fish. Brer Fox said that he caught them. Brer Rabbit asked where, and Brer Fox told him down at the creek. Brer Rabbit asked how, because in those days everyone was monstrous fond of minnows.

Brer Fox sat down on a log and told Brer Rabbit that all he had to do to get a big mess of minnows was to go to the creek after sundown, drop his tail in the water, sit there till daylight, and then draw up a whole mess of fish. Those he didn't want he could fling back. Right there's where Brer Rabbit made a big mistake, because he went out that night to go fishing. The weather was sort of cool, so Brer Rabbit fixed

himself something to drink and set out for the creek. When he got there, he picked out a good place, and he squatted down and let his tail hang in the water. He sat there, and he sat there, and he drank his drink, and he thought he was going to freeze, but, by and by, day came, and there he still was. He made a pull, and he felt like he was coming in two, and he made another jerk, and lo and behold, where was his tail?

It had come off, it had, and that's what made all these bobtailed rabbits you see these days, hopping and skedaddling through the woods.

84

Mr. Terrapin Shows His Strength

One night, Miss Meadows and the gals gave
a candy pulling, and so many of the neighbors came in response to the invitation that they
had to put the molasses in the wash pot and boil
it on the fire in the yard. Brer Bear helped Miss
Meadows bring in the wood, Brer Fox tended the fire,
Brer Wolf kept the dogs off, Brer Rabbit greased the
bottom of the plates to keep the candy from sticking,
and Brer Terrapin climbed up in a chair and said he'd
watch and see that the molasses didn't boil over. They
were all there, and they weren't playing any pranks,
either, because Miss Meadows put her foot down and
said that when they came to her place, they had to
hang up a flag of truce at the front
gate and abide by it.

Well, while they
were all sitting there
and the molasses
was boiling and bub-
bling, they got to talking
mighty big. Brer Rabbit said
he was the swiftest, but Brer
Terrapin just rocked in the
rocking chair and watched
the molasses. Brer Fox said

he was the sharpest, but Brer Terrapin just rocked along. Brer Wolf said he was the wildest, but Brer Terrapin rocked and rocked along. Brer Bear said he was the strongest, but Brer Terrapin just rocked, and he kept on rocking.

By and by, he sort of shut one eye, and said, "It looks to me like the old hardshell is nowhere alongside this crowd, but here I am, the same one who showed Brer Rabbit that he's not the swiftest, and I'm the same one who can show Brer Bear that's he's not the strongest.

Then they all laughed and hollered, because it looked like Brer Bear was stronger than a steer. By and by, Miss Meadows asked how he was going to prove that he was stronger than Brer Bear.

"Give me a good strong rope," said Brer Terrapin, "and let me get in a puddle of water, and then let Brer Bear see if he can pull me out!"

They they all laughed again, and Brer Bear said, "We've got no rope."

"No," says Brer Terrapin, "and neither have you got the strength," and Brer Terrapin rocked and rocked in the rocking chair, and watched the molasses boiling and blubbering.

After a while, Miss Meadows said that she'd loan them some rope, and, while the candy was cooling in the plates, they could all go to the brook and see Brer Terrapin carry out his project. Brer Terrapin wasn't much bigger than the palm of your hand, and it looked mighty funny to hear him bragging about how he could outpull Brer Bear. But they got the rope after a while, and they all set out for the brook. When Brer Terrapin found the place he wanted, he took one end of the rope and gave the other end to Brer Bear.

"Now ladies and gents," said Brer Terrapin, "you go with Brer Bear up there into the woods and I'll stay here, and when you hear me holler, then's the time for Brer Bear to see if he can haul in the slack of the rope. You take care of that end," said he, "and I'll take care of this end."

They all set out and left Brer Terrapin at the brook. When they'd all gone, he dove down into the water and tied the rope hard and fast to a huge root, and then he rose up and gave a whoop.

Brer Bear wrapped the rope around his hand, winked at the gals, and with that, he gave a big jerk, but Brer Terrapin didn't budge. Then he took both hands and gave a big pull, but Brer Terrapin still didn't budge. Then he turned around and put the rope across his shoulders and tried to walk off with Brer Terrapin, but it looked like Brer Terrapin didn't feel like walking. Then Brer Wolf helped Brer Bear pull, but it was just as if he hadn't, and then they all helped him, and while they were all pulling, Brer Terrapin hollered and asked them why they didn't take up the slack. When Brer Terrapin finally felt them quit pulling, he dove down and untied the rope.

By the time the others got down to the brook, Brer Terrapin was sitting at the edge of the water, just as natural as anybody, and he said, "That last pull of yours was a mighty stiff one. A little more, and you would have had me. You're monstrous strong, Brer Bear, and you pull like a yoke of steers, but I sort of had the advantage on you," he said.

Then Brer Bear's mouth began to water after the sweets. He said he expected the candy was ready, and off they all went after it.